Dedicated to some old and new friends:
Addoley D.
Kelly D.
Isabel W.
Monika P.
Jean C.
Linda Z.
and Erica E.

THIS IS A BORZOI BOOK PUBLISHED BY ALFRED A. KNOPF

Copyright © 2017 by Karl Newsom Edwards

All rights reserved. Published in the United States by Alfred A. Knopf, an imprint of Random House Children's Books, a division of Penguin Random House LLC, New York.

Knopf, Borzoi Books, and the colophon are registered trademarks of Penguin Random House LLC.

Visit us on the Web! randomhousekids.com

Educators and librarians, for a variety of teaching tools, visit us at RHTeachersLibrarians.com

Library of Congress Cataloging-in-Publication Data
Names: Edwards, Karl Newsom, author, illustrator.
Title: I got a new friend / Karl Newsom Edwards.
Description: First edition. | New York : Alfred A. Knopf, [2017] |
Summary: "A little girl and her new puppy get to know one another." –Provided by publisher
Identifiers: LCCN 2016005552 (print) | LCCN 2016031286 (ebook) |
ISBN 978-0-399-55700-2 (trade) | ISBN 978-0-399-55701-9 (lib. bdg.) |
ISBN 978-0-399-55702-6 (ebook)
Subjects: | CYAC: Dogs–Fiction. | Animals–Infancy–Fiction. | Friendship–Fiction.
Classification: LCC PZ7.E25635 Ig 2017 (print) | LCC PZ7.E25635 (ebook) |
DDC [E]–dc23

The text of this book is set in 29-point Loose.

The illustrations were with pencil and watercolor and then refined digitally.

MANUFACTURED IN CHINA
May 2017
10 9 8 7 6 5 4 3 2 1

First Edition

Karl Newsom Edwards

# I Got a New Friend

ALFRED A. KNOPF    NEW YORK

I got a new friend.

She's kind of shy.

At first, she was sort of scared.

But she got used to me.

# My friend likes to play outside.

She messes up the house
and sleeps on the furniture.

She's stinky,

but that's okay.

She gets lost . . .

# and found!

# Sometimes she gets dirty

and needs a bath.

# My friend is a sloppy eater,

but she can wash her face all by herself.

She's really, really noisy,

except when she's asleep.

She needs lots of hugs, kisses, and even more kisses.

She can be a lot of work, but I love her.

She's my little girl!

# How to care for your new friend:

Help each other.

Share.

Keep clean.

Play together.